Mia
Time to Trick or Treat!

HarperFestival is an imprint of HarperCollins Publishers.
Mia: Time to Trick or Treat!
Copyright © 2012 by HarperCollins Publishers

Library of Congress catalog card number: 2011927584
ISBN 978-0-06-210011-5
Book design by Sean Boggs
12 13 14 15 16 CWM 10 9 8 7 6 5 4 3 2 1 ❖ First Edition

Mia
Time to Trick or Treat!

HARPER FESTIVAL
An Imprint of HarperCollinsPublishers

By Robin Farley • Pictures by Olga and Aleksey Ivanov

"I love Halloween!" Mia says. "I love to carve pumpkins. I love to dress up! But the best part is trick or treating with my friends!"

"Do you know what you want to be?" asks Mia's mom, Mrs. Cat.

Mia spins and twirls. "A ballerina, of course!" she says. "Maybe Anna and Ruby and I could dress up as matching ballerinas!"

Mia waves to her mom and runs up the stairs of the school. Anna and Ruby are waiting.

"Happy Halloween, Mia!" says Ruby.

"I thought of a great costume idea!" says Mia. "We could all be matching ballerinas!"

"Perfect!" says Anna. "Let's be blue ballerinas. Blue is my favorite color."

"What about green?" says Ruby. "I like green best."

But Mia does not want to be a blue ballerina or a green ballerina.

She wants to be a pink ballerina.

"I have a better idea," Mia says. "Let's be pink ballerinas!"
Anna and Ruby frown. Ruby looks at her shoes. Anna shakes her head.
"We don't want to wear pink," Anna says. "I want to wear blue. Ruby wants to wear green."

The girls don't know what to do. They want to match, but they can't agree on a color. Before they can decide, the school bell rings. The three dancing friends glide into the classroom.

"Hello, class!" says Miss Monkey. "In honor of Halloween, we will be making paper jack-o'-lanterns today!"

Mia, Anna, and Ruby draw and cut and glue.

Mia holds up her work. "Look at my pink jack-o'-lantern!" she says. "Doesn't it look great?"

"Yes, but I do like my blue pumpkin! Isn't it pretty?" asks Anna.

"Very pretty," says Ruby. "But not as pretty as my green one!"

Miss Monkey walks by and sees all of the pumpkins. "What a dazzling display of colors, girls! They look especially great together. I'll hang them on the wall, all in a row!"

After school, Mia, Ruby, and Anna go to Ruby's house.

"Happy Halloween!" Ruby's mom says. "Are you all ready to go trick or treating?"

"Sort of," says Anna.

"We want to be matching ballerinas," says Ruby.

"But we can't agree on a color," says Mia.

"I see," says Mrs. Giraffe. "Don't worry. I'm sure you will work it out. Would you like to help me decorate these cookies before you start on your costumes?"

"Oh yes!" says Anna. "Do you have a blue apron? After all, blue is the best color."
Ruby picks up the green food coloring. "Let's make the frosting green," she says.
"Green is so beautiful."

The girls decorate every cookie until the kitchen is filled with pink, blue, and green.

"These cookies look great!" says Mrs. Giraffe. "Oh, but look at the time! Let's all wash our paws and hooves. Mrs. Cat is on her way to take you trick or treating!"

"Oh no!" says Ruby. "Our costumes aren't ready! How can we all wear the color we want and still match?"

Mia thinks for a minute. She looks around the kitchen. She looks at the rug. She looks at the walls. She looks at the flowers. Then she sees Ruby's backpack.

"I know!" says Mia. "We can wear blue and pink and green!"

"What do you mean?" asks Anna.

Mia points to Ruby's tie-dye backpack.

"We can make tie-dye costumes just like my backpack!" says Ruby.

"Great idea, Mia!" says Mrs. Giraffe, smiling. "We'd better get to work!"

The girls dip and dye their costumes, then practice their pliés in the living room while the costumes dry. Soon, the leotards and tutus are ready, and the girls try them on.

"Oh! They are beautiful!" says Anna.

"They are the best Halloween costumes ever!" says Mia.

The girls dance outside in their pink-and-blue-and-green costumes.
All of the neighbors smile as the bright ballerinas prance by.
"Beautiful costumes!" says Mrs. Giraffe.
"So colorful!" says Mr. Hippo.

"What a great idea!" says Mrs. Cat.
Mia leaps. Ruby twirls. Anna pliés.

The ballerinas dance to Miss Bird's Dance Studio. Mia knocks on the door. "Trick or treat!"

When Miss Bird opens the door, she gasps. "Oh my! What delightful dancers! I've never seen such exquisite tutus!"

The dancers twirl and spin.
"Bravo!" sings Miss Bird.
What a wonderful Halloween!

Mia and her friends are getting ready to trick or treat and they need your help!
Use the stickers to create colorful costumes, just like they did in the story!